To Craig with love
from Granny & Grandad Bill
Christmas 1999.

THE SCHOOLBOY,
THE CURATOR AND
THE TIME MACHINE

D1350929

THE SCHOOLBOY, THE CURATOR AND THE TIME MACHINE

MICHAEL FORSTER

Illustrated by
Terry McKenna

An imprint of Kevin Mayhew

First published in 1996 by
KEVIN MAYHEW LTD
Rattlesden
Bury St Edmunds
Suffolk IP30 0SZ

0 1 2 3 4 5 6 7 8 9

ISBN 0 86209 844 0
Catalogue No 1500052

Front cover designed by Veronica Ward
Edited by Stephen Haddelsey
Printed and bound in Finland by WSOY

This book is dedicated to every 'David'
who has to face up to a 'Goliath'.

CONTENTS

CHAPTER 1

Just Any Old Morning

'Come on, Davey! Get a move on or you'll be late.' Davey thought Dad must have an obsession with Being On Time. He wondered whether there was some reason for that. Had he been kept waiting for his feed when he was a baby, and developed a complex about it? Or perhaps it was just one of those silly hang-ups grown-ups get – like locking the front door and then having to open it again to check that the gas is turned off.

Ever since Davey could remember, every morning had been the same. First, Mum would wake him up and say, 'Now don't forget to wash properly and brush your teeth.' Then she would complain that he was too long in the bathroom! Dad would say that children had no consideration, and Granddad would talk about the war when they had to manage with only five inches of water in the bath – not that

Davey even wanted a bath anyway. Then, just as he was sitting down for breakfast, Dad would say the famous words: 'Come on, Davey! Get a move on or you'll be late.' And Mum would add, 'Jenny's already gone.' Jenny would have! Ever since she moved up to middle school, she'd become a real bore. She always set off early to get there on time, and then at night she'd lock herself away and do her homework. By the time she'd finished it was Davey's bedtime. They used to have fun together once, but now she only spoke to Davey to boss him around. Anyone would have thought she was ten years older, not just two. 'That's the trouble with girls,' Davey thought. 'Once they get to A Certain Age, they get boring.'

Mum and Dad seemed to think she was some kind of angel. 'Why can't you be more like Jenny?' they used to say to him. There were times when Davey wished big sisters had never got past the design stage.

This morning, life downstairs was especially tense. Mum had taken up one of her Good

Causes, and Dad didn't approve of it. 'I don't see that you need to spend all day at some protest rally or other,' he said. 'It won't change anything, anyway.'

Mum didn't answer. 'It's an exciting day today, Davey,' she said. 'Have you forgotten the class outing?'

Davey hadn't forgotten the class outing. They were going to visit a museum and he thought it was naff. 'What's the point of learning about dead people?' he said. 'Why can't they teach us about exciting things like cars and computers?'

'That's it!' said Mum. 'You can leave the rest of your toast – put your coat on and let's get you to school.'

So far the day had been just like every other day, and so it continued until lunch. Then Mr. ('Pompous') Purdey got the class together and gave them a little talk. 'Now remember,' he said, trying hard as usual to sound very important but not quite managing it, 'I'm responsible for you – so don't let me down. You're representing the school. I want no bad

11

behaviour, be polite to the museum staff and don't go wandering off. Understand?'

'Yes, Mr. Purdey,' the children chorused.

'Miss Thompson is coming with us,' Pompous continued. 'I shall lead the way, naturally, and she will supervise you from behind. Come along children,' and they set off. Every so often, Pompous would turn round to ensure that nobody had fallen down a manhole or got lost in a sweet shop. And whenever there were a lot of people around to hear, he would call out something like, 'Come on, children, heads up, shoulders back – keep them in order, Miss Thompson!' Miss Thompson, who was quite human for a teacher, smiled politely but made no reply.

When they got to the museum, they were on the wrong side of the street. 'Wait here,' said Pompous, 'until I've stopped the traffic.' With that, he stepped majestically into the road and held up his hand. Now it was just bad luck that the driver of the approaching car was looking in his mirror checking that his hair was tidy.

When he looked at the road again, he was horrified to see Pompous standing right in front of him. The driver slammed on the brakes and there was a loud screeching of tyres as the car skidded to a halt just in time. The car behind him didn't quite manage it, though, and neither did the one behind that. The air was filled with the screeching of tyres, the thud of metal on metal and a pretty tinkling sound as glass that had once shone proudly on the fronts of headlights broke into a thousand pieces and landed on the road. The drivers got out angrily and started arguing, waving their arms around, shouting and blaming each other, while the children did their best to pretend they were not with Pompous. Some looked intently into shop windows; others squatted down to tie up shoelaces that were perfectly well tied to begin with, and Davey and his friend Edwin Harrington started pointing up to the sky and having a conversation about a non-existent aeroplane. Pompous decided to Do The Right Thing – which for him at that moment meant get the heck out of there. 'Come on, children,' he called out. 'We mustn't be late at the museum.'

Miss Thompson helped to see the children across and then said, 'I'll be with you in a moment, Mr. Purdey – I think one of us should try to help those people.' Pompous didn't seem very pleased, but seeing that Miss Thompson had a Determined Look on her face he gathered the children together and ushered them into the museum, muttering things about drivers not looking where they were going and apparently thinking that he had behaved entirely sensibly.

Mr. fforbes, the museum curator, was a little different from the other exhibits. He was quite small and slim, and looked as though a breeze would blow him away. Wisps of white hair floated around the top of his head like an undisciplined halo. He wore a charcoal grey suit, half drab and half shiny, with trousers that stopped just a little too far above his shoes; round his neck was a winged collar and a frayed blue bow tie, and perched in front of his right eye was a monocle, which made that eye look larger than the left and added to the eccentric appearance of its owner.

'Ah, of course! St. Ethelred's school. 'Yes, yes, yes, I remember. I'm Mr. fforbes, the Curator, and Miss Wilkins is my assistant. She will show you around, and if you have any questions please don't be afraid to ask.'

Davey wasn't afraid,

'Please sir, are you God? Only, we've been told that God created everything. Isn't that right, Mr. Purdey?'

'You Stupid Child!' roared Pompous. 'He's the curator – not the Creator. I do apologise, Mr. fforbes. *Most* of our children are quite intelligent.'

'Oh, please don't apologise,' chuckled Mr. fforbes. 'Children must ask questions, you know! No, children, I'm the person in charge of the museum – that's what a curator does.'

With that, Mr. fforbes shuffled off, giggling to himself and repeating, 'God! God! Oh, dear me! That's a new one!'

Pompous was very red and did what he always did when he was embarrassed – he told the children off. 'Now, children, whatever that old – er – the curator said, I don't want any more silly questions. Just behave yourselves. Now, Miss Wilkins, do you think we should start?'

Miss Wilkins was very nice – young as adults go, pretty if you like that sort of thing, and as near human as grown-ups ever get. Davey wondered what she was doing working with Ancient Relics. Pompous put on his 'perfect gentleman' act, rushing to open the door to the first room which was full of strange bits of metal. Miss Wilkins began to explain what they were, but Davey wasn't listening; he'd noticed a door in the corner with a sign saying 'Strictly no entry.' Now if there's one way guaranteed to get Davey to do something, it's to tell him not to. And this was *strictly* telling him not to! Pompous was staring in rapture at Miss Wilkins and had forgotten all about the class. So Davey quietly sidled over to the door and found to his delight that it was unlocked. Without anyone noticing, he pulled it open and slipped through.

CHAPTER 2

The Thing in the Cellar

In the light from the main room, Davey could see a staircase going down into a dark cellar. What could be down there? Probably Egyptian mummies – bodies preserved from thousands of years ago. He didn't fancy stumbling onto one of those, alone in a dark cellar. Then he thought of Pompous and the other Ancient Relics upstairs and decided this couldn't be any worse. Gingerly, he started down the steps toward the cellar, looking out for nasty creepy crawlies which he might use to frighten Pompous later, and eventually he reached the bottom. Turning the corner, he found himself in a room about the size of a classroom, completely dark except for the light coming through a very high window. Stacked around the walls were a lot of the kinds of things you would expect to find in a museum – boring things, Davey would have said – including what seemed to be quite a collection of broken pottery. Davey was about to go back when he stopped and stared. Could that be what he thought it was? Surely not! But it was: a small open-topped sports car! Davey was fascinated. What was anything so exciting as this doing in a museum? How on earth had they got it down here? He went a little closer, and found that this was a very strange car indeed. It seemed to be made up from all kinds of bits and pieces. On the boot was a logo saying 'Triumph Herald 13/60' while the front was from an MG. The doors had apparently been rescued from an old Hillman Imp and certainly didn't fit very well, and the windscreen didn't belong to any of those but sat there in an embarrassed sort of way held on by a few self-tapping screws. The whole contraption was painted – somewhat inappropriately, Davey thought – in British Racing Green.

As he looked, Dave noticed something else that was strange about this little car. It didn't seem to have a steering wheel. Instead, in front of the driver was a screen and a keyboard rather

like the computers they had at school. 'Wow!'
thought Davey. 'Now here's something worth
looking at.' He climbed into the car and looked
around for the computer switch. He couldn't
find it, but noticed that there was what looked

like an ignition key in the dashboard. He also noticed that the car was quite different from the one his parents had, in that there was no gear lever, no foot pedals and no handbrake. The car must be completely controlled by this computer. What a turn-up: the two things that Davey found most exciting in the whole wide world – cars and computers – both together in this dingy cellar! Perhaps museums weren't such boring places after all. Davey wondered what would happen if he turned the key. Would the car start? Or would it blow up and wreck the museum? There was only one way to find out, so Davey reached out, held his breath and turned the key in the dashboard.

Nothing happened.

For about ten seconds.

Davey was just about to get out of the car when he noticed that the computer screen was beginning to glow. It got brighter and brighter, with strange shapes and shadows appearing from the centre and growing larger to fill the screen before disappearing to be replaced by something else. Davey watched this in fascination. 'Well,' he thought, 'it's a heck of a screensaver!' Then the images stopped and a message appeared.

Time/space co-ordinate software,
copyright © Prof. H. I. Hipperwattle
Last co-ordinates
BC1015/0305/0933/3124N/3503E/+0032
F4 for list of last six co-ordinates
F5 to set new co-ordinates
RETURN to return

What could all that mean? Davey thought there was only one way to find out. So, holding his breath in excitement, he reached forward and pressed the RETURN key.

Meanwhile, upstairs, Mr. fforbes was getting cross. 'Oh dear, dear, dear!' he fussed as he picked up another empty sweet wrapper. 'Why can't these Dreadful Children be more careful!' Now the children of course should not have been eating sweets, let alone dropping the wrappers, but Pompous Purdey was far too busy paying attention to the delightful Miss Wilkins to notice what they were doing – while Miss Thompson of course was still outside, sorting out the scrap metal and bad tempers left by his earlier misadventure.

As Mr. fforbes huffed and puffed about the Dreadful Children, he glanced toward the cellar door and froze with horror. Somebody had opened it! The staff had orders never to leave the door unlocked; there was supposed to be strict security in the area. Why, if anyone ever discovered the cellar's dreadful secret the result could be horrible. It could change the Whole Course Of History and end Civilisation As We Know It. Mr. fforbes turned towards his office to get the key, but as he did so he froze in this tracks. He heard a sound coming from the cellar, and it was a sound he dreaded! With a turn of speed quite amazing for a Man Of His Age (which Davey had secretly guessed might be two hundred and four) Mr fforbes galloped across the room toward the basement door.

Davey was sitting in the car absolutely fascinated by the noises it was making. It began with a whirring sound which gradually got louder and was joined by a strange, irregular popping as though someone had thrown a handful of bangers onto a bonfire. Then came a regular 'thumpety thump', like an enormous heart beating and finally a wail like an ambulance siren. As each new sound started, the earlier ones got louder as well, and soon the cellar was reverberating with noise like a mad fairground. Davey was frantically trying to turn off the computer, but it wouldn't respond to any keystrokes at all and try as he might the ignition key wouldn't turn. The noise got louder and louder, and Davey thought everyone in the town must be able to hear it. Just as he was thinking that he had done a Very Silly Thing, and probably ought to jump out, the figure of Mr. fforbes appeared at enormous speed through the doorway, shouting furiously but unable to make himself heard above the din. Realising it

was too late to stop the machine, he threw himself into the passenger seat beside Davey. He was only just in time; as they sat there together, the room began to spin around them. There was no possibility of jumping out now: the spinning was getting faster every moment.

CHAPTER 3

The Incredible Thirty-Century Video Rewind

Davey and the curator hung on grimly to their seats as the room and everything around them accelerated. The cellar disappeared and the scenery changed as if someone was rewinding a giant video. As the movement got faster, Davey could make out less and less detail, but he caught glimpses of people walking backwards at enormous speed, ships rising out of the sea, aeroplanes flying in reverse, rain being sucked up into clouds – and then it all became a blur and he could see only a grey mist with flashes of colour. Davey didn't know whether he was excited or terrified! 'What's happening?' he asked Mr. fforbes, breathlessly.

'"What's happening?"' echoed the curator. 'We're travelling back in time, you Stupid Boy, that's what's happening. When will children like you learn not to interfere with Things

That Don't Concern You?'

So that was it! A time machine!

'But where did it come from?' Davey asked. 'I thought time travel hadn't been invented yet.'

Mr. fforbes was very cross with Davey, but he'd always believed children should be encouraged to ask questions. 'It was invented in 1980 by Professor Horatio Ignatius Hipperwattle,' he explained. 'When the government found out, they had it hushed up.'

'Why?'

'I should have thought that that was patently obvious!' answered Mr. fforbes impatiently. Then seeing that it clearly wasn't obvious to Davey he explained. 'If people learned to travel in time, it would be disastrous. They would be able to alter the course of history – and we don't want Ordinary People doing that, now do we!'

Davey noticed a twinkle in his companion's eye, and was about to ask what he meant when the curator went on. 'Now listen. When we stop, you are not to get out of the machine,' he said. 'We shall simply use the stored co-ordinates in the databanks to take us back to our own time and place.'

Davey was horrified. What a waste! This was the adventure of a lifetime, and he had no intention of simply turning back when he got to the other end.

'You can go back if you like,' he said. 'I'm going to look around.'

'You just listen to me,' hissed Mr. fforbes. 'This is a very dangerous thing to play around with. You might change the Whole Course Of History. Why, you could even change things so that you didn't exist any more. Do you want to do that?'

Davey thought that was silly, but Mr. fforbes insisted.

'Do you know where all your most distant ancestors came from?' he asked. 'No, of course you don't! What if somebody got killed, or married the wrong person? You could be interfering in all kinds of Things You Don't Understand. So we're not going to stay.'

Then Mr. fforbes looked thoughtful, and reached to open the glovebox. 'I suppose it's better to be safe than sorry,' he muttered, as he took out what looked like two digital watches, put one on his own wrist and gave the other one to Davey. 'Put this on, just in case, but don't do anything silly. You're to stay in your seat and we're going straight back.'

Davey decided to change the subject.

'What happened to Professor Hipperwattle?'

'If you must know,' said the curator, 'they gave him a lot of money to keep him quiet and sent him to work at the BBC, hoping he would just get lost there. An awful lot of people do, you know.'

Before Davey could ask the curator what he meant by that, he noticed that the fast rewind was slowing down and he could make out a few more details. It was still going very fast indeed, and he could only catch glimpses, but it seemed that they were going somewhere exciting. Gradually, it slowed down more and things got clearer. Davey saw strange people in weird costumes. It looked a little bit like some of the historical adventure programmes he'd seen on the television. Because it was all going backwards it was difficult to work out what was really happening, but there seemed to be battles being fought, houses burning, animals stampeding, all the things you see on good videos – except that it wasn't a video. Davey was quite nervous about actually being there, in the middle of all this, and was thinking that perhaps Mr. fforbes was right about going straight back, when the scene slowed right down and they came to rest. They seemed to be on a rough hillside track about three metres wide; judging from the footmarks and wheel ruts, it had been beaten down by the passing of horses and carts, as well as human feet. On one side the hill rose steeply; it was very rocky and almost barren, except for occasional sprigs of gorse or bracken. On the other side, rows of vines simply dripping with lovely ripe grapes covered the ground which sloped gently for perhaps ten or twenty metres and then dipped sharply to the valley below. The whole scene shone in the dewy light of a summer early morning, and from high above, where the hill sloped out of sight, the air was filled with the songs of birds staking out their territory for the coming day.

'Wow!' exclaimed Davey. 'I wonder where we are!'

'*When* we are, more to the point,' Mr. fforbes corrected him, reaching for the key, 'but I'm not staying to find out. Let us restart the computer and return with the utmost haste.'

The words fell on deaf ears. Davey was staring around in amazement at the beautiful scene, and had forgotten all about the nerves he had felt earlier. Before Mr. fforbes could stop him, he was out of the time machine and heading for one of the vines.

'Come here, you Stupid Boy!' shouted Mr. fforbes, frantically.

'I won't be long,' Davey called. 'I just want some grapes to take home.'

'We have no time for that,' fussed the curator, impatiently. 'We have got to get out of here before…'

Davey wasn't listening. He had heard something much more exciting than Mr. fforbes's voice. Faintly but clearly, the sound carried on the light breeze to where he was standing. It was beautiful, exciting, and somehow familiar. It wasn't the music itself which Davey recognised, but there was something about it. Of course! The rhythmic beat, the thundering of the drums and the strident sound of what must have been trumpets; and along with all of that the steady, rhythmic pounding of marching feet. It was a parade!

Now if Davey had been thinking carefully he might have connected those marching feet with the battle scenes he'd glimpsed just before the time machine stopped. But that was Davey's trouble. He didn't think. As soon as he heard the sound, he forgot about the grapes, and the time machine, and even about Mr. fforbes. Especially about Mr. fforbes! He had to go and see the parade! So, before the astonished eyes of the horrified curator, Davey dropped the grapes he had just picked, turned away and ran off in the direction of the sounds.

'Hey! You, boy! Come back here! You really are a Very Stupid Boy!'

It was no good; Davey was already out of earshot. Mr. fforbes wondered what he should do. He knew how to operate the machine, of course, so he could just go back. But he couldn't leave Davey. Apart from getting himself into trouble, Davey was quite likely to do Something Silly and change history. No, there was nothing else for it. Mr. fforbes would just have to go after the boy. His mind raced. He had to catch Davey as soon as possible, but should he leave the time machine? What if it was discovered? What if it was damaged? They had to be able to get back. No, he would have to hide the time machine first, even if it took him longer to catch up with Davey. Mr. fforbes decided to try and push the machine in between the vines. It wasn't much but it would have to do; so he put his shoulder behind the rear wing and began to push. As the wheels slowly started to turn, Mr. fforbes huffed and puffed to himself, 'Oh, that Stupid Boy! This really is a Fine Mess! Why can't children just keep away from Things That Don't Concern Them!'

CHAPTER 4

The Terror of the Twelve Tribes

For the moment, Davey had forgotten about the time machine, the curator and everything else that he really should have remembered. To his right, the vineyard had given way to gently sloping open fields separated from the road by a ditch. The verge before the ditch was lush green grass, covered in a rash of yellow and white flowers. The hill rising to his left gradually became less barren, with occasional bushes and shrubs clinging by their roots to the unhelpful soil. In front of Davey, a gazelle appeared, obviously running away from the band. It stopped for a moment and looked at Davey, before leaping the ditch and darting off across the meadow. Davey was so intrigued by the gazelle that he almost didn't notice the snake that crossed his path. He needn't have worried though: the snake was far too concerned with trying to evade a hungry mongoose to take any notice of Davey. What a wonderful place this was!

As the sound of the band drew nearer and nearer, Davey's legs were going faster and faster with his heart pumping furiously to keep up. He wondered what kind of parade it was. Was it a carnival? Perhaps it was a circus! The sounds got louder: the trumpets were sounding fanfares while the drums were rat-tat-tatting a rousing march rhythm, and the tramping of feet made the ground shake. It had to be a military parade. Davey wondered what kind of soldiers they were. After all, he didn't even know what century this was. As that thought struck him, it jogged his memory in the nick of time and some words Mr. fforbes had said flashed into his mind.

'Why, you could even change things so that you didn't exist any more. Do you want to do that?'

Davey's blood ran cold at the very idea, and his run slowed down to a trot at the same time as his imagination started working faster. In running off like that, he had done a Very Silly Thing! What if these soldiers were unfriendly?

What if they mistook him for an enemy? What if they were cannibals and Roast Boy was one of their favourite meals? Davey's trot slowed down to a walk, and then he stopped. The music was very loud by now, and he knew the band must be just round the next bend in the path. Davey slipped quietly into the ditch at the side of the track and tried desperately to hold his breath and keep his head down. He thought his pounding heart would be sure to give him away.

The ground shook as the marching feet came nearer and the trumpets and drums filled the air with stirring music. Although Davey was scared, he was also excited and couldn't resist raising his head just enough to take a peek. The mixture of feelings became more intense as the column of soldiers rounded the bend and came into view. He must have gone back in time quite a long way, for he had never seen soldiers like these ones. The man marching in front looked as though he was probably an officer. The first thing Davey noticed about him was his shiny breastplate which reflected the sun, and what

seemed to be a kind of kilt, swinging as he
marched. Round his waist was a leather belt
which joined to another one crossing from his
shoulder, and this supported the weight of his
sword which bounced rhythmically against his
thigh in time with his marching and the playing
of the band. On top of his head was a metal
helmet with a large plume made of brightly

coloured feathers and in his hand he held a short spear with which he beat time for the band.

The band members were obviously less important than the officer, and did not qualify for the protection of breastplates. They were dressed in bright scarlet tunics which came down to just above the knees, and round their heads were purple sweatbands knotted at the back. They marched in twos. The first six pairs were drummers, with different sized drums made by stretching animal skins over hollowed out branches of trees. Behind them marched two pairs of bandsmen shaking maracas which seemed to have been made from dried fruit skins filled with stones. Then came the wind instruments: all kinds of strange looking contraptions; some seemed to be just animal horns, while others looked a little bit like the kinds of trumpets and horns Davey had seen in the school orchestra. And as the soldiers marched they blew for all they were worth – with a lot more enthusiasm than skill in some cases.

Finally (or so Davey thought) behind the

band came about fifty foot soldiers. They were not so well dressed as either the officer or the band, and seemed to be wearing mainly leather clothes, roughly cut from animal skins, to protect the top halves of their bodies, with quite short kilts leaving their legs free to move quickly in battle. On their heads, some had rough and ready helmets made from leather, while others went bareheaded. They seemed a very motley bunch – not at all like the soldiers Davey was used to seeing – but he knew they were soldiers because they were armed to the teeth with a variety of weapons; Some had spears, others heavy wooden staves, and each had a dangerous looking sword hanging from his belt. A number of them had scars from earlier battles, and a few wore eyepatches. Altogether, they looked a very threatening gang of cut-throats and Davey was glad he had had the sense to hide – until he noticed that he was not alone in the ditch. Normally, Davey wasn't afraid of spiders, but this was different from the ones he saw at home. It was quite large, a yellowish brown colour, and had beautiful paler markings on its furry legs and body. Davey knew that in some parts of the world spiders were poisonous, and this one didn't seem happy to share its home but was crawling toward him in a very threatening way.

As soon as the squad of soldiers had passed, Davey scrambled out of the ditch just in the nick of time. The spider, having ensured that the intruder did not seem to be coming back, decided that honour was satisfied and returned to its lair. Davey now felt that this adventure was getting just a little too adventurous and was going to make his way back, following the soldiers at a safe distance. However, he had moved too soon. Spider or no spider, to have waited a little longer would have been a Very Sensible Thing to do, for just as he was emerging from the ditch Davey came face to face with the rear guard. And what a rear guard it was. Davey couldn't believe his eyes! He tried to run away but it was too late; he had been seen, and before he could take two paces an enormous hand reached out and grabbed him by his arm. Davey struggled and kicked, but it was no use. He was roughly dragged back and brought face to face with the most terrifying man he had ever encountered; even more terrifying than the school inspector who had come round last week and told him that his work was Very Unsatisfactory, and that he Could Do Better!

The man must have been fully three metres tall! Added to that, he had a large bronze helmet on his head, matching the bronze breastplate which covered his enormous chest and slung round his waist was a sword which must have been taller than Davey.

The giant had his hands full, for as well as Davey in his right hand he was holding in his left a long spear which must have been about as thick as a rugby post and had a vicious looking pointed iron tip. His eyes glared suspiciously at Davey, and when he spoke his bushy beard seemed to become a cloud emitting great claps of thunder.

'Well, well, well!' boomed the giant. 'And just who might you be?'

Davey was surprised. Since he was fairly obviously in a foreign country, and a completely different time, he wondered how it was that the man spoke the same language, but decided that perhaps this was one time when asking questions really wasn't a good idea. In any case, he could hardly speak, he was so terrified, so he confined himself to stammering out, 'I-I-I'm Davey. Er, Who are … you?'

The giant looked angry and Davey thought he must have done another Very Silly Thing. He had, because however much famous people may complain about being recognised, there's nothing more likely to offend them than when people say, 'Who are you?'

'"Who am I"?' roared the mountainous warrior, and the breeze he caused ruffled Davey's hair. Then the thunderous voice began to rise in a terrifying crescendo. '"Who am I"? I'm the Terror of the Twelve Tribes, the Scourge of Saul, the Great One of Gath; I'm the one whose very name makes the Israelites tremble and weep; and you ask who I am! I'll tell you who I am, you Puny, Pathetic, Pallid-faced Pipsqueak. I'M GOLIATH.'

CHAPTER 5

Davey and Goliath

Mr. fforbes had managed to get the car between the vines, but only just. One of the front wheels was jammed and try as he might he couldn't shift it; and he didn't dare start it up again in case he disturbed the stored data in the computer, which would be vital for getting them home. 'Well,' he thought, 'it will do as long as people don't look too hard – how fortunate that Horatio painted it green. With any luck I'll find that Stupid Boy and we can be back here and off home before it's discovered.'

Mr. fforbes just had to go and find Davey, partly because he was afraid Davey might interfere in history, but also because in the short three thousand years that he had known the boy, he had actually begun to like him. In fact, despite his apparent impatience with them, Mr. fforbes was really very fond of children; it was just that they got too much for him at times. As he used to say to some of his friends. 'I really like children – but I couldn't eat a whole one.'

The sound of the approaching band which had lured Davey away was now getting closer, and the curator knew he would have to move quickly. He started along the path where Davey had gone. On and on he went, and still there was no sign of the boy, and the sound of the band was drawing nearer. He was only too well aware of the danger should he be discovered, and like Davey he looked for somewhere to hide. He didn't very much fancy the ditch with its multi-legged inhabitants, so clambered up the steep hillside and crouched among the boulders. There wasn't a great deal to do while he waited for the band, so he passed the time worrying. What if they had already found Davey? What might they have done to him? It was a great relief when the column passed him without any sign of Davey. Presumably, the boy had had the sense to hide. Then another dreadful thought struck him. What if the soldiers found the time machine? Well, there was nothing to be done except hope. With a bit of luck, they would be concentrating on marching in step and not looking too hard at the surrounding scenery. Mr. fforbes decided that the best thing to do would be to carry on looking for Davey. He was just about to break cover when he heard a familiar voice.

'Let me go, you big bully,' the voice was saying. 'I'm *not* a spy.'

'That,' said a bigger and stronger voice (obviously from a bigger and stronger body), 'is what they all say. You might as well stop struggling. No-one gets away from Goliath of Gath.'

'Oh dear, dear me!' thought Mr. fforbes. 'This is a Fine Mess we're in!'

Round the bend in the path came the giant, with Davey firmly in his grasp. Goliath was holding Davey by the arm so that his feet were barely touching the ground. Davey was struggling and kicking, but it was no good; he could not escape. Mr. fforbes was angry and fearful both at the same time. He wanted to rescue Davey but knew that he could never fight Goliath. So he stayed hidden until they had passed and then, keeping carefully out of sight, followed to see where they went.

Davey was extremely frightened. Apart from being afraid that this dreadful giant might kill him – and even eat him – Davey knew that, even if he survived, he would have to get back to the time machine and find Mr. fforbes or be stuck in this strange world for ever. When they got to where the time machine had been, he didn't see it hidden away in the vines but thought Mr. fforbes must have left him and gone home. So that was that. He was stuck here for ever. What a Terrible Thought!

Goliath was still trying to find out who Davey was and where he was from. 'How long have you been spying on us?' he demanded.

'I haven't,' Davey yelled. 'I don't know anything about you.' That wasn't true, of course, because Davey had read all about Goliath and the Philistines in his Bible, but he wasn't telling Goliath that!

'Just like those cowardly Israelites,' Goliath spat, scornfully. 'They send out a snivelling boy to do a man's job. Next thing we know, they'll be sending children into battle!'

Davey kept quiet. He had calmed down now, and was trying to think of a way out. One thing he knew was that no other Philistine was as big as Goliath. So he might have more chance to escape when he was handed over to their normal-size soldiers.

Before long, the main track turned sharply right and began to wind up the hill, but Goliath took Davey off to the left, to the camp where the rest of the Philistine army was based; there seemed to be soldiers everywhere. Davey was surprised by the camp because he had always thought that the Philistines had been uncivilised savages, but this place was very highly organised and even attractive. The tents were decorated with beautiful pictures, and in the open spaces were sculptures which Davey thought must be statues of the Philistine gods. Even though he didn't approve of home-made gods, he had to admire the skill of the people who had made them. Then he realised he was being dragged towards a large and highly decorated tent with its own guards outside. The sentries moved aside to let Goliath pass – well, they would, wouldn't they? – and Davey was dragged inside the tent to stand before a person who he knew must be the Philistine king.

The king looked at Davey from under bushy eyebrows, and appeared very puzzled. 'Well, I have to hand it to you,' he said. 'You're different from the usual spies we get here.'

Davey's heart leapt. Perhaps that was his opportunity. 'Please, Your Majesty,' he said, 'I'm not a spy. I mean, if I was I'd be disguised as an ordinary Philistine – wouldn't I?'

The king seemed impressed. 'You know, Goliath,' he said, 'He's got a point. No spy would go around drawing attention to himself in ridiculous clothes like that.'

Davey was glad he wasn't at a school that made the pupils wear uniform. If these people thought his best jeans, *Save the Whale* sweatshirt and

designer trainers were ridiculous, what would they have thought of flannel shorts and a blazer! Still, as things seemed to be going his way he didn't argue.

'That might be what he's hoping you'll think, Your Majesty,' Goliath answered. 'Just like the treacherous Israelites! Anyway, whether he's a spy or not, he's obviously not one of us.' Then his voice brightened horribly. 'Shall I kill him now?'

'No, no, no!' exclaimed the king. 'You did well to bring him in alive. He might know something.'

That was a new one for Davey. When he was at school, Pompous was always complaining that Davey didn't know anything at all. But what did these people want him to say?

'How many soldiers have the Israelites got?' asked Goliath.

'What's the range of their catapults?' asked the King.

'Have they found anyone to fight me, yet?' Goliath followed up.

Davey was frightened again now, and couldn't think what to answer. The king got impatient.

'Take him away!' he shouted. 'And bring him

back when you've made him talk.'

Goliath dragged Davey away to a compound and tied him to a stake in the ground. Then he bent down and grinned menacingly. 'In a few hours it'll be midday,' he said. 'Only mad dogs and tourists go out in the midday sun in these parts. With that pale skin of yours, you'll fry!

When you've had enough, and you're willing to talk, just let us know.'

And Goliath went away, chuckling nastily to himself.

Davey didn't know what to do. He couldn't tell them anything that would convince them. Since Mr. fforbes had taken the time machine away, there wouldn't be any proof of his story. What was going to become of him? Even as he thought it, he began to feel hotter. The sun was beginning to rise higher in the sky and there was no shade or cloud anywhere.

What was he going to do?

CHAPTER 6

Curator to the Rescue!

The midmorning sun – and the thought that it would get even hotter by midday – was making Davey wish that Professor Hipperwattle had never been born! There were other things he wished as well. He wished that he'd not given his teacher such a hard time. After all, the poor fellow couldn't help being pompous any more than Davey's sister Jenny could help being a girl! And perhaps Dad might have a point about Being On Time. Now that he wasn't going to see any of them any more, he decided they were all a lot nicer than he had ever realised.

Davey's thoughts were interrupted by the voice of Goliath, and however loud it had seemed to be before he had obviously only been muttering! A great, resounding thunderclap reverberated around, echoing and re-echoing like a C.D. player in a biscuit tin.

'Come on, you miserable Israelites, send

someone out to fight me. Or are you toy soldiers all too frightened to take on a real warrior?'

Davey knew that everybody's attention would be on Goliath, and thought this might be his chance to escape. He pulled at the ropes and tried to slip his hands through, but it was no use. The ropes were too tight. Then a bony hand appeared from behind him and clamped itself firmly over his mouth and Davey heard a strangely familiar voice.

'Right, you Stupid Boy, just for once in your life, listen to your elders and do as you're told.

When I take my hand away, keep quiet. Do you understand?'

Davey was overjoyed. Mr. fforbes hadn't deserted him after all.

'*Do you understand?*'

Davey nodded – as best he could with his head in Mr. fforbes's vicelike grip – and felt the pressure of the fingers ease against his mouth. Mr. fforbes transferred his attention to the ropes, and Davey heard him muttering under his breath as he struggled to undo the knots, all the time expecting the soldiers to come back. After a few minutes, Davey whispered, 'What about your monocle?'

'I told you to be quiet!' hissed the curator, crossly. 'Anyway, I can see perfectly well – it's the knots that are too tight.'

'Where is it?' Davey insisted.

Mr. fforbes was losing his patience. 'If you must know, you Stupid Boy I put it in my pocket for safety. It's a valuable antique – d'you know that it once belonged to…'

Davey was really desperate by now. 'Use it to

burn through the ropes,' he said.

The light dawned on Mr. fforbes. Of course! Perhaps this wasn't quite such a Stupid Boy as he had thought! He removed his monocle from his pocket and focused the hot sun onto the ropes. Soon there was a smell of burning and smoke began to rise. Just as Davey thought he couldn't hold back his coughing any longer, he felt the ropes weakening and with a huge effort managed to break them apart. As soon as he was free, he and Mr. fforbes set off, keeping low and moving stealthily between the tents. The camp was empty; everyone had gone to watch Goliath taunting the Israelites.

Suddenly, Mr. fforbes stopped and stared. 'Well!' he exclaimed. 'Upon my soul!' Davey turned and saw that the curator was standing still and gazing in rapture at a water pitcher outside the tent. It stood about a metre high and was decorated with beautiful slip-work; figures of men, women and animals. 'Well,' Mr. fforbes exclaimed excitedly, apparently forgetting that they were in mortal danger. 'I never thought I should see such a perfect example of one of those.'

Davey couldn't see what all the fuss was about. When you'd seen one old vase, you'd seen them all as far as he was concerned. He was much more interested in the probability of the soldiers returning.

'Come on,' he said,' or they'll find us again.'

'What? Oh, yes, of course,' said Mr. fforbes, absently, but he still stood there gazing at the pitcher. Then what Davey had feared happened. One of the soldiers had obviously got bored with watching Goliath challenge the Israelites – especially since no one had ever accepted the challenge so far – and decided to go back to the camp. The soldier came round the corner and stopped to stare in amazement at the bizarre looking figures before him – luckily, he had not seen Davey before or they would *really* have been in trouble. His brief hesitation was Mr. fforbes's opportunity, and what Davey saw next taught him that there is often more to people – and even museum curators – than meets the eye.

Mr. fforbes did not panic, but approached

the soldier with a confident smile. 'Good day to you,' he beamed. 'I do not believe we have met. I'm the new entertainments officer round here.'

The soldier was as surprised to hear that as Davey was. 'Entertainments Officer,' he said. 'I didn't know we had one of those.'

'Didn't know?' Mr. fforbes pretended to be cross. 'No wonder no one came to my show last night. How do they expect me to maintain morale among the troops if they don't tell anyone about me. Just a moment – what's that?'

Before the bemused trooper could stop him, Mr. fforbes reached up and produced a ping-pong ball from behind the man's ear.

'How did you do that?' gasped the soldier.

'Oh, that's nothing,' said the curator, airily. 'This trick's *much* better.' From his jacket pocket he took a pair of small metal rings which he showed to the fascinated soldier. 'Look at those,' he told him, and see if you can find any breaks in them. No? Quite sure they're solid? Then how about this?' Mr. fforbes triumphantly held one of the rings aloft, with the other dangling from it.

The soldier grasped the rings and looked at them closely. He simply couldn't work out how it was done! Somehow, the two solid rings had become linked together, and he couldn't find a break in either of them.

Here,' said Mr. fforbes kindly. 'Let me help,' and he took the rings from the soldier and handed them back to him separately. The poor man was completely overwhelmed. Still unable to find any breaks in the rings he stared at them in fascination, clashing them together in a vain attempt to link them. Mr. fforbes thought this was a good chance, and he whispered an order to Davey.

'Run, boy! Run! I'll catch up.'

Davey understood, but was reluctant to leave the curator there on his own. After all, his new friend had not deserted him when he was in trouble – even though it was his own fault. So he just stood still, staring at Mr. fforbes and trying to decide what to do.

The opportunity was gone before Davey could collect his thoughts. 'It's a great trick,' said the soldier. 'What else d'you do?'

Mr. fforbes gave Davey an exasperated look before answering the question. 'Oh, all kinds of things,' he said, casually picking up a few pebbles and juggling with them, 'but you'll have to come to the show – then you'll be able to see the dancing, as well.'

The trooper's eyes lit up. 'Dancing? You mean…'

'Oh, of course,' Mr. fforbes assured him. 'I have a very beautiful assistant who's a wonderful dancer. I'm sure she's around somewhere. Look, why don't you get a few of your comrades together and I'll try and find her and meet you here.'

The soldier hesitated. 'I'm not sure,' he began, but then had second thoughts. 'Well, it would be better than watching Goliath shout at those cowardly Israelites. Okay, you're on – I'll get them.'

As the soldier turned and walked away, Mr. fforbes whispered to Davey, 'We were lucky there – we got a dull one to deal with – now as soon as he's out of sight, we run. And do try to get it right this time. Whatever happens, don't stop or look back. Got it?'

Davey nodded, and he did exactly as he was told. As the soldier disappeared round a tent, Davey took to his toes. He could hear the curator huffing and puffing behind him. Just as he had been told, he didn't look back but kept on going as fast as he could.

Behind him, Mr. fforbes was trying very hard to catch up, which to be honest would have been difficult enough for him even if they had

not been running uphill. As he ran, the curator gasped, 'Wait! Come back! Oh, you Stupid boy! Not again!'

By the time Davey had to pause for breath, they were well clear of the camp, but could still hear Goliath hurling taunts and insults at the Israelites. Their frantic run had taken them round and slightly up the hillside, so they were well shielded from view. Davey got his breath back as Mr. fforbes caught up with him and stood there with his eyes bulging and his mouth gaping as his lungs fought for air. Davey looked at his friend with admiration. 'That was brilliant!' he said. 'Where did you learn to do conjuring tricks?'

'If you must know,' gasped the still breathless Mr. fforbes, stuffily, 'my family has a long tradition in the performing arts. If you knew your history you would have heard of my grandfather, Marco the Mystery Man, of music hall fame.' He paused for a moment to catch his breath. 'However, more importantly for now, it appears that I also have a better sense of direction than you do. Precisely where would you say that the time machine is?'

Davey was stuck, but he wouldn't admit that to Mr. fforbes. 'Oh, I think it's over there,' he said, pointing further ahead. 'It must be just over that ridge.'

'On the contrary,' retorted Mr. fforbes, 'It's right over there.' And he pointed back toward the Philistine camp. 'You Stupid Boy, you have done it again.'

'Done, er, done what again?' Davey faltered.

'Thanks to your irritating habit of doing first and thinking later,' replied the curator, 'we have escaped on the wrong side of the Philistine camp. Now what are we going to do, I wonder!'

Davey didn't see what all the fuss was about. 'We can go back and work our way round to the other side, can't we?' he said.

'It looks as though we'll have to,' replied the angry curator. 'And if we don't get captured again, we'll probably get lost. Have you any idea how big that camp is? You really have got us into another Fine Mess!'

CHAPTER 7

The Decisive Battle

Davey was grateful for having been rescued, and his regard for the curator had increased very much, but he thought he was being unfair. 'You said run,' he objected. 'You didn't say which way.'

'Because I mistakenly credited you with the sense to know,' retorted Mr. fforbes. Then, seeing Davey's crestfallen face he softened. 'Not to worry,' he said, weakening for a moment and ruffling Davey's hair. 'The important thing is we're together again.'

Davey thought that was really nice of Mr. fforbes, and gave him a big smile. Mr. fforbes looked embarrassed. 'Can't have Stupid Boys messing around with Things That Don't Concern Them!' he mumbled, gruffly.

Just at that moment, there was a resounding cheer, loud enough to drown even Goliath's rantings. The noise seemed to be coming from the other side of the ridge, so Davey and the curator crept forward to see what was causing it.

When they came to the ridge, they peered over, careful to stay out of sight, and found themselves looking down into a valley with the Philistines on their left and a second army on their right. It was at this point that another Terrible Thought struck Davey. He'd never given his name much thought until now, but might it be – could it be – no, it was too ridiculous to contemplate. But then, what had Mr. fforbes said earlier? 'You might change the course of history so that you don't exist'! Perhaps it could be! Maybe he was the 'David' who was to fight Goliath. And if the course of history was changed then he wouldn't exist any more. Oh, what was he to do?

As these thoughts were going through Davey's head, he realised that the cheers were all coming from their right – which must be the Israelites. Goliath had stopped shouting and was standing with his cavernous mouth gaping wide open in amazement. Following his gaze, Davey saw the cause of all the excitement. A

small figure – a boy who from that distance looked about Davey's age and size – had emerged from the Israelite camp. So *that* was the David of the Bible story! What a relief! Davey had had one brush with Goliath already, and was very glad not to have to have another.

The boy walked very calmly and resolutely toward the centre of the valley; he wore a simple piece of animal skin, slung over the shoulder and tied around his waist. In his hand he carried a slingshot. As the boy crossed the valley, he stopped and stooped down to put his hand in the stream that was flowing gently past him. They could not see from that distance what he was doing, but Davey knew that he was choosing some stones for ammunition. As he straightened up, Goliath recovered from his shock and started shouting again.

'I knew it!' he bellowed. 'First child spies, and now child warriors! Haven't you got any Real Men in Israel?'

'I'll show you what's what,' replied a shrill voice. 'God has helped me fight wolves and lions, and he won't have any trouble with you.'

Davey and Mr. fforbes were watching all this intently. They had both read the story of David and Goliath, but actually to be here, in the Holy Land, ten centuries before Christ, witnessing the event live was an enormous thrill. Still, we all have to make sacrifices, and Mr. fforbes took hold of Davey's arm.

Come on,' he said. 'We've got to get back to the time machine, and while everyone's watching this we must Grasp The Opportunity.'

Davey wanted to see the battle, and thought fast. 'According to the Bible story,' he said, 'there won't be a Philistine camp to get round in a few minutes. We're better lying low until it's all over.'

Mr. fforbes secretly wanted to stay as well, and anyway Davey had a point. 'That is correct,' he said thoughtfully. 'Very well, but please keep quiet, and stay out of sight.'

Goliath had started down the mountain. He was very angry indeed. After all, he was the feared champion of Philistia, undefeated in countless head-to-head contests. There could hardly be any greater insult to him than for the enemy to send out a child to fight him. The giant charged down the mountain, roaring madly as he went, and stopped about fifty metres from David. He raised his enormous spear and aimed it at the shepherd boy, but he was too late. David had already loaded his sling, and started to swing it round. As the spear came up, so David let the stone go. Although they were too far away to see much detail, Davey and Mr. fforbes knew that the stone had found its target right in the middle of Goliath's outsize forehead.

For what seemed like an eternity, the giant stood still with his spear poised. Then his raised hand began to sag and his knees to buckle; the spear which had been ready for launching at David crashed to the ground just ahead of Goliath. When the giant also hit the grass it was impossible to know whether the tremor which the two time-travelling spectators felt was caused by the giant's fall or by the foot-stamping and shield-beating of the cheering Israelites. The noise was simply beyond description. Davey thought it must be heard all over the world, and even in the twentieth century! The Israelites were absolutely overjoyed, and they were going to let everyone know about it. The Philistines, on the other hand, were totally silent in disbelief. The mighty warrior who had killed and terrorised for them throughout the region, who had despatched fierce, hardened fighters as though they were children, had been defeated by a child! As the watching pair observed all this, they saw the boy David go up to Goliath and take out the fearsome looking sword from the giant's belt. Holding the sword in both hands, and staggering a little under its weight, David brought the weapon down on Goliath's neck completely severing the head from the body. At that point, Davey felt sick. Goliath had been a bully, and Davey had always enjoyed reading this ending of the story in his Bible, but seeing it happen in real life was a different matter. He could not

help feeling sorry for the fallen giant, and for his people who had now been totally humiliated. And as David paraded the severed head in front of the Israelites, Davey found himself becoming angry. Mr. fforbes seemed to sense how Davey was feeling and put a kind hand on his shoulder. 'That's the problem with history,' he said. 'Reading about it's one thing, but being part of it is quite another.'

As the curator spoke, the awesome reality of the victory seemed to dawn on both armies. The Israelites drew their swords and rushed toward the Philistines, who were so terrified that they simply turned and fled. Mr. fforbes motioned Davey to take cover, and they slipped back below the skyline. 'Better wait here,' he said gently. 'We should be safe until it's all over.'

Davey was quite glad not to watch. He could hear the pounding feet, the screams of pain and terror as Philistines were trapped and killed, and then his nostrils caught a familiar smell. Something was burning. The Israelites had set fire to the beautiful tents of the Philistines, and soon a massive plume of smoke marked the place where they had been.

Davey and the curator continued to lie low on the blind side of the hill until the battle was over. Finally, Mr. fforbes said, 'I think it should be safe to leave now.'

Very cautiously, they made their way back towards where the camp used to be, until they rounded the mountain and looked across toward a scene of horrible devastation. The camp itself was just a charred mess, and as they walked towards it they came across the bodies of soldiers, some with their weapons still sheathed, so sudden had been the change of fortune. Mr. fforbes put an arm round Davey's shoulder and they walked through the ruined, deserted and eerily silent camp toward the place where they had left the time machine.

Soon they came to the fork in the road, and began to feel happier at the prospect of going back home. 'I hid the machine between the vines,' said Mr. fforbes, 'so it should be safe.' But he was wrong. The machine was not to be found. All they could see were some muddy scars on the ground, where it had been dragged out of its hiding place, and some fresh tracks made by horses' and people's feet. What on earth could have happened to it? And what was going to become of Davey and the curator?

CHAPTER 8

Another Parade

'Where's it gone?' asked Davey, in amazement.

The curator looked as though he was about to make a very angry reply, and then saw Davey's face and changed.

'I don't know,' he said, 'but we'd better find it. And the most fruitful course of action would probably be to follow those tracks.'

Davey was listening intently – but not to Mr. fforbes He had heard a familiar sound coming from above them. 'Just a minute,' he said. 'Listen – I can hear a band again. It's coming from up there.' And he pointed up the rocky slope.

This time, Mr. fforbes did get angry. 'Just for once will you pay attention? It was you and your ridiculous chasing after bands that got us into this Fine Mess in the first place. We have got to get the time machine back.'

Sometimes, Davey wondered how Mr. fforbes had ever got such a responsible job as his when he couldn't see the Perfectly Obvious when it was right in front of him! 'That's what I meant...' he began to say, but Mr. fforbes interrupted him.

'Good! I'm glad we agree about something! Now shall we go?'

He still didn't understand! Davey decided it was time to put his foot down. 'I'm not moving from here,' he said in a Very Determined Voice, 'until you listen to me.'

Mr. fforbes put on his Stern Face, and was about to add his Not-To-Be-Trifled-With voice to it when something in the look on Davey's face stopped him. 'Oh, very well,' he sighed. 'What is it?'

'Elementary, my dear fforbes,' Davey began – and ducked just in time. 'It won't be the Philistine band – so it's probably the Israelite victory parade – and if it's the Israelites that have found the time machine – and if they think it belongs to the Philistines...'

'Really, boy,' fussed the curator, 'We haven't got time for chasing Red Herrings. Let's get moving. The tracks go that way.'

Now Davey was really getting angry with the curator. 'But who says the road goes in a straight line?' he shouted, stamping his foot as he did so.

Mr. fforbes went quiet for a moment, and thought very hard. 'You know,' he said thoughtfully, as though he had worked it out all by himself, 'it just might be that the track zigzags up the hillside, in which case we could take a short cut up through the rocks and meet up with the parade on the other side. Yes, that's it. What a good thing I thought of it.'

Davey rolled his eyes upward, shrugged and sighed deeply. That's the trouble with adults. They don't think children have got anything worthwhile to say, and when a child has a good idea they take all the credit themselves! Still, the important thing was that he'd got through.

'Well, don't just stand there, boy – we've got to get going! Must I think of everything?'

With that, Mr. fforbes grasped Davey's hand and set off up the hill at what was really quite a remarkable pace for a Man Of His Age – even if he did come from a show-business family.

Up and up they scrambled, the curator grasping rocks and shrubs with one hand and holding Davey firmly with the other. His feet seemed to have eyes in them as they found the best footholds, and the only signs that their owner was struggling were the panting and puffing sounds emerging from his lips and an extra shine on his forehead. Although he wouldn't have admitted it to anyone, Davey would have been quite nervous on a climb like this on his own, but he felt completely safe with his older friend, who he was beginning to recognise was a man of rare talents.

As they climbed the sound of the band got louder, showing that they were going the right way. Davey wasn't very impressed; he thought the Philistine band he first met had played a lot better, but he didn't say so, partly because he didn't want to annoy Mr. fforbes any further and partly because he was completely out of breath.

Still Mr. fforbes dragged him upwards,

scrambling over boulders and occasionally dislodging loose rocks which went bouncing and rattling down the hillside. And all the time he still seemed to have some breath left to mutter, 'Got to get the machine back. Mustn't let them play around with it.'

Gradually, the ground began to level out as the rocky terrain slowly gave way to rough grass, and they found themselves once again on a broad beaten track, but this time on the other side was a dense, dark forest. By now, the sound of the band and the tramp of what sounded like thousands of feet was becoming deafening. Quickly, Mr. fforbes ran across the track, still clutching Davey's hand, and found cover among the trees. He was just in time to avoid being seen by the bandmaster as the parade swung into view. The bandsmen were blowing their horns, beating their drums and cymbals for all they were worth, and just behind came a party of Israelite soldiers. They were singing and cheering as they went, and seated on their shoulders was the young lad who had earlier defeated Goliath. Now that he could observe him closely, Davey saw that David was probably just a few years older than himself, but still small and very young to be the Hero Of The Moment. Just behind David, seated on a magnificent chestnut horse, came a person who could only be the king. King Saul looked absolutely splendid in his armour, the plume of his helmet blowing in the wind and the sun glinting on his breastplate. Even Mr. fforbes was impressed. 'Doesn't he look majestic?' he whispered to Davey.

Yes,' Davey admitted, 'but it's a funny thing. I didn't see him going to fight Goliath. He sat in his tent while David did it.'

Mr. fforbes did not reply. The procession had changed. First came a party of Israelite walking wounded, some supporting themselves on sticks or being helped by comrades, others carrying stretchers with their more seriously wounded comrades on them, and all struggling to keep up with the forward party. Then behind them came a bedraggled, sorry looking collection of

Philistine captives. Davey recognised some of the bandsmen he had seen before, not now marching proudly but staggering along, their tunics torn and bloodstained, heaving at ropes with which they were pulling wagon loads of looted treasure. The midday sun was now almost fully up, and they sweated and groaned with the effort, but their captors did not seem to care and kept them moving by lashing them with whips.

Davey and the curator stayed concealed in the trees as they watched the procession go past. Davey was sad to see these once proud warriors now so humbled and shamed. He wondered what would happen to them when the procession reached its goal and they were no longer needed to pull the wagons.

Suddenly, Mr. fforbes put a hand on Davey's shoulder and signalled to him to keep quiet, before pointing back along the column of men and wagons. Davey followed the curator's finger and saw a large, powerful horse drawing a sturdily built wagon on which he could plainly

see a British Racing Green bonnet, a pair of shiny headlamps and the famous eight-sided MG badge. They had found the time machine. The problem was, so had the Israelites; and after the trouble they had gone to it didn't look very likely that they would be ready to give it back.

Mr. fforbes kept a tight grip on Davey's arm as the machine drew level with them; not that he needed to, because Davey had no intention of tangling with the large and brutal looking guards walking each side of the wagon. Eventually the last stragglers had passed and Davey and Mr. fforbes waited until they had got well ahead before stealthily following, still keeping in the cover of the trees. The hilltop was now levelling out and the track sloped very gently as it wound its way round, first left and then right, following the outline of the hill.

Davey just had to say it, even though he knew he'd probably get into trouble. 'You're a very good climber for an ol – a Man Of Your Age,' he said.

He was right. He did get into trouble.

'If you must know,' sniffed the curator, 'I am precisely forty seven and a half years old – which is hardly geriatric – and I climb in Snowdonia most holidays, so that little hill presented no difficulties whatsoever.'

Davey wondered whether there were any more hidden facets to this man, but before he could say anything else the curator shushed him and pointed ahead.

A town had come into view and it was obvious that that was where the procession was aiming. As they drew near, people came out from the houses and cheered the army home. Some children and women jeered at the prisoners and hugged the returning soldiers. Others went anxiously looking for husbands and fathers, and some started to cry when they realised the bad news. The Israelites had won the battle, but there was still grief for very many people.

Davey and the curator watched all this from the shelter of the wood, and saw the victory parade gradually disappear into the town.

'What do we do now?' asked Davey.

'"What" we do is simple,' answered the curator. 'It's "how" that's the problem. We've got to get into that town without being noticed. And I don't think that will be at all easy.'

CHAPTER 9

The Prowler in the Forest

Davey was both nervous and excited. If they went into the town, what might they find? The Israelites hadn't seemed to him to be any less cruel than the Philistines, and he didn't fancy getting captured by them. There again, he was actually beginning to find this historical stuff quite interesting. He wondered what kind of houses there were, how people would be dressed, whether children would be made to go to school. Did they have people like Pompous and Miss Thompson? He didn't think they would have *anybody* like Mr. fforbes!

Then he realised that his friend was muttering again.

'Got to get into that town! There must be some way of getting in without being noticed.'

'Of course there is!' said Davey. 'What we need is a disguise.'

'Brilliant!' exclaimed Mr. fforbes, sarcastically.

'And just where do you propose to find one?'

'Shouldn't be too difficult,' Davey answered. 'You could just sneak in when no-one's looking and steal some clothes from people's washing lines.'

Mr. fforbes was horrified. 'Just what kind of person do you think I am?' he demanded. 'I do not "sneak" anywhere, and I certainly will not steal from washing lines – assuming they have such things here. Why, if Mrs. fforbes ever found out...'

It had not occurred to Davey that there even was a Mrs. fforbes. He tried to imagine what she might look like, but was interrupted by the curator who started muttering again.

'We'll just have to wait here until night,' he said. 'Then we should be able to get into the town.'

Now it was Davey's turn to be horrified. 'Stay here 'till night? We can't do that – my dad'll kill me. He's got a real thing about Being On Time.'

'If we go into that town in broad daylight,'

retorted his elder, 'the Israelites might do it for him. Anyway, as long as we get back to the museum at the time we left, details about the time here will be irrelevant.'

Then a Terrible Thought seemed to strike the curator. 'You aren't thinking of telling about this when we get back, are you?'

'Well, er...'

To be truthful, Davey had been thinking what a wonderful story he was going to have to tell. None of his friends had ever done anything like this.

'Because if you are you'd better think again,' said Mr. fforbes using his Stern Voice. 'That machine is an Official Secret, and do you know what happens to people who give away Official Secrets?'

'Yes,' thought Davey, ' Mum says they get rich,' but he knew better than to say it out loud.

The curator was a typical adult – fussing and worrying, and having secrets – but right now he was more concerned with the present – or was it the past – well, you know what I mean. How were they going to get out of this Fine Mess?

The sun was now directly overhead, and it was very hot indeed. Davey remembered what Goliath had said. 'Only mad dogs and foreign tourists go out in the midday sun. With that fair skin you'll fry!'

'I think you're right,' he said to the curator, trying to sound very wise. 'Anyway, to go out in that sun would be a Very Silly Thing to do.'

Mr. fforbes smiled. To be honest he hadn't thought of that; he had been more afraid of looking conspicuous in their strange clothes. He knew Davey was right, though. 'We'll stay here in the shelter of the trees until nightfall, and then we'll try to find the time machine.'

So they retreated into the wood. Davey thought this might be the time to ask the question which had been nagging at him all day.

'I don't understand,' he said, 'how it can be that everybody speaks our language.'

'Oh, that's easy,' responded the curator. 'They don't – they speak ancient Hebrew, here.'

That, of course, just made it worse, not better!

'But we've been talking with people, Davey insisted – and they *do* speak English.'

'No they don't,' Mr. fforbes assured him. 'That's STUART.'

Davey looked around, but didn't see anyone else there.

'Who?' he asked

'STUART,' repeated the curator. 'Simultaneous Translator for Universal Application in Recorded Time.

'I think I'll just say STUART,' said Davey, 'but what-who is it-he?'

'It's on your wrist,' explained Mr. fforbes. ' You remember – I told you to put it on before you left the time machine.'

'Oh, of course,' said Davey, and blinked a couple of times.

'It seems to me that you need some sleep,' Mr. fforbes observed, and Davey had to admit his friend had a point. He couldn't work out why he was feeling tired. Mr. fforbes explained.

'It's only midday here,' he said, 'but it was afternoon when we left our own time, and we've been here for some hours now. You're jetlagged! Why don't you lie down and go to sleep?'

If anyone had told Davey he would sleep on an adventure like this, he would have said that they were round the bend; but it had been an exciting time, and he was very, very tired.

'Don't worry,' said Mr. fforbes. 'I'll keep watch, but you'll need to be wide awake later on.'

So Davey stretched out under a tree and fell fast asleep.

Next thing Davey knew, he was being woken up by Mr. fforbes who again had a bony hand firmly over his mouth. 'Don't make a sound!' the curator whispered. 'Someone's coming.'

Davey looked around, and it took him a few moments to remember where – and when – he was. The wood was darker now, and he guessed it was late afternoon or early evening, and he could clearly hear the rustle of feet in the undergrowth. The two adventurers sat quite still and listened, and then their blood ran cold as they heard the unmistakable sound of a dog rummaging and sniffing around. As they were wondering what to do next, a furious barking began, and the dog started to run toward them.

Davey never ceased to be amazed at Mr. fforbes's agility. The curator jumped to his feet, picked Davey up as though he were made of cotton wool and effortlessly lifted him up high enough to gasp the branches of the tree. As Davey heaved himself onto the bough the curator scrambled up after him, just in time. Out of the bushes around them came the largest dog Davey had ever seen. He didn't recognise the breed, but it looked like a cross between a rottweiler and a lion as it jumped up against the tree trunk, barking furiously.

'Hey! King! What's the matter, boy?'

At first, Davey couldn't see where the voice was coming from, until the bushes parted and a face appeared. It was a good face, with a kind of grandfatherly quality about it. The mouth was hardly visible, obscured by a white moustache which came right round to join up with a long,

flowing beard. Above the moustache was a large red nose, and either side of that the brightest pair of twinkling blue eyes Davey had ever seen. The face was topped with more white hair – not wispy like the curator's but thick and bushy – and somewhat untidy.

The face came closer, followed by the rest of the body emerging from the undergrowth. The voice was as gentle as the eyes. 'What's the matter, boy – what have you found? Well, bless my soothsaying soul!'

The eyes, which had travelled up the tree to see what was exciting the dog, now popped open even wider and seemed to jump out from the face in astonishment.

'Well I'll be a Philistine cowherd!' the man exclaimed. 'What have we here?'

Davey and Mr. fforbes did not reply. They were staring in terror at the dog.

Suddenly the old gentleman roared with laughter. 'Surely you're not frightened of King? He makes a lot of noise but doesn't do a lot – that's why I call him King! The worst he's likely to do is lick you to death!'

Mr. fforbes was not impressed. 'I'll thank you, sir, to keep that four-legged menace away from us. Have you any idea of the kind of diseases that can be transmitted through being licked by a dog ?'

The old man looked puzzled. 'I'm not sure I follow you,' he said, 'but why don't you come down here? I'm getting a crick in my neck.'

The man reached up and helped Davey down. Immediately, the dog was upon him, pinning him to the ground, growling horribly and baring its teeth just inches away from his face.

Chapter 10

Another Fine Mess

The enormous jaws came closer and closer. The eyes seemed to gleam horribly, and the mouth opened wider. Then, just as Davey thought he would faint with terror, a large, rough, wet tongue started to lick him frantically. At the other end of the animal a long tail was wagging excitedly, and the growl changed to little squeals of pleasure. Davey was not only relieved but overjoyed to find a friendly face – even if it did have bad breath and no conversation.

'Come on, King – give the poor lad a bit of air!' The old gentleman pulled the dog away and held it as Mr. fforbes gingerly came down from the tree.

'Well, I'll be a camel's grandfather!' exclaimed the stranger. 'What crazy outfits! Why, if I had to go around like that I'd expect my tailor to pay *me*! Now where are my manners! My name's Samuel – prophet, judge and trusted adviser to His Majesty King Saul. And who might you be?'

Davey was relieved. He'd read about Samuel, and knew he was a good man. 'I'm Davey,' he said, 'and my friend is called fforbes.'

'*Mister* fforbes, if you don't mind,' put in the curator, stuffily.

'Mistaforbs, Mistaforbs,' repeated Samuel. 'Oh, well, my old Dad was called Elkanah, but he managed to live with it, so I'm sure you can.'

Samuel looked again at their clothes. 'Weird,' he said. 'Truly, wondrously weird! Would you have anything to do with that wacky chariot the army brought in today?'

Davey and Mr. fforbes looked at one another. It really seemed as though they had no choice. Mr. fforbes drew Davey aside.

'I think,' he said, 'that it would be expedient to divulge such information as is pertinent to the situation.'

Davey was lost! 'I don't know about that,' he replied, 'but I think we should tell him.'

Mr. fforbes looked tired. 'Precisely!' he said. 'Leave the talking to me.'

Then he turned back to Samuel.

'We are travellers from a far country, many months' journey to the West,' he explained. 'The "chariot", as you so aptly call it, is our means of transportation, and it is vital that we secure immediate and unhindered possession of it.'

Samuel gaped.

''We've come a long way, and we need the chariot to get home,' Davey translated.

'Oh, why didn't you say so before?' Samuel replied.

'You mean you'll help us?' asked Mr. fforbes, excitedly.

'Not on your fig-picking life, Misty Baby!' the prophet answered.

'Why not?' Mr. fforbes was becoming impatient.

'These are dangerous times,' came the reply. 'How do I know you're not spies?'

'Really!' exclaimed the curator. 'Is everybody here obsessed with espionage?

'Spying,' translated Davey.

'Thank you,' said the prophet. 'Look, I'd really like to help you because I've taken a bit of a shine to you if the truth be told. But it's just more than my life's worth.'

'It might be more than your life's worth not to,' answered Davey, and to Mr. fforbes's horror he continued, 'Does King Saul know you've already anointed the shepherd boy as king of Israel?'

Samuel's face turned almost the same colour as his beard.

'H-h-how did you know that?' he faltered.

'Back where we come from,' Davey replied, 'my friend is known as Mystic Mistaforbs, the

Wondrous Wizard of the West. And I'm his pupil – he's teaching me all he knows'

Mr. fforbes had now caught on and, although he didn't approve of blackmail, he couldn't help a sneaking admiration. He joined in the conversation.

'Now don't misunderstand,' he said, soothingly. 'We wouldn't dream of telling the king, but the trouble is that all our secrets are hidden away in our chariot, and if the king ever found out how it works…'

The curator's voice tailed off leaving Samuel's imagination to fill in the details.

'And if I help you get your chariot back you'll go?' he asked, hopefully.

'No question about it,' answered Mr. fforbes, 'but first we need to get into the town and we can't go in like this.'

Samuel had recovered from his fright, and decided to trust these strangers. Something told him that they were honest, and even if they weren't he didn't have a lot of choice really. That chariot had to be got rid of – not for his own sake, of course, but for the good of the nation. Samuel didn't see anything else for it: he had to get these strangers into the garrison where the chariot had been taken.

The curator and the prophet began to discuss ways in which they might achieve this. Samuel suggested that he could first get them a change of clothes and then introduce them to the king as his friends. 'Saul and I are real friends,' he said. 'He trusts me.'

Mr. fforbes thought that was a splendid idea, until Davey asked, 'What will the king do to you after we've stolen the ti – I mean, er, chariot?'

Samuel hadn't thought that far ahead. The king would be looking for someone to punish, and since they were Samuel's friends he'd probably qualify for a nice lingering death. Samuel didn't fancy that idea at all, so he and Mr. fforbes put on their thinking caps again. Every time they came up with a plan, it had the same weakness. 'It's no good,' said the curator wearily. 'We're just going to have to find our own way of getting in, without involving

Samuel.'

For a moment, all was silent as the three of them thought very hard. Then Samuel's face lit up.

'By the holy beard of Moses!' he exclaimed. 'I've got it! Mind you, it's a bit risky but I think it might work.'

Mr. fforbes looked desperate. 'Whatever we do will incur an element of risk,' he said. 'What is your idea?'

'It's like I said, Misty Baby,' crowed Samuel delightedly (ignoring the curator's irritated scowl), 'I'm the king's trusted adviser. I think I should do my duty, and hand you over.'

Mr. fforbes exploded angrily. 'I've never heard such a Ridiculous Idea!' he snapped. 'Do you want to ruin everything?'

Samuel looked at Mr. fforbes in a very knowing way, and said, 'It's really very simple. The king wants to know about the chariot, and you're the one who can tell him. You need it to get home, and for that you've got to get into the garrison. I really think in this case honesty is the

Best Policy. I must do my duty.' And he gave
Mr. fforbes a very exaggerated wink and tapped
the side of his nose with his forefinger as if to
say, 'Know what I mean, mate?'

Mr. fforbes clearly didn't know at all. Samuel
turned to Davey.

'He's not very bright, your friend, is he?' he
commented.

Davey didn't know what Samuel was getting
at, either, but he didn't want to look as silly as
Mr. fforbes – although in actual fact, he would
have found that difficult anyway.

Suddenly, Mr. fforbes's face lit up, and he
said, 'Oh, I see! Of course!'

'Well I'll be a donkey's Godfather,' exclaimed Samuel. 'I do believe he's got it!'

'Yes, yes, of course!' muttered Mr. fforbes. 'That's it! Risky as you say, but it just might work, and we can't afford to waste any more time.' Then he raised his voice, to try to cover the tremor of excitement and fear, and said, 'Samuel, do your duty!'

'Right!' said the prophet. 'You just wait here – we shouldn't be long. Come on, King. Here boy!'

And with that, he disappeared through the rapidly darkening wood with the dog romping along beside him.

'Oh dear, dear dear!' fussed the curator. 'I hope we're doing the right thing. If not, we'll really be in a Fine Mess!'

CHAPTER 11

Cornered, Captured and Caged

Jake, the sentry on duty at the barracks, was fed up. It wasn't fair: everyone else was enjoying the celebrations now that the Philistines had been beaten. His friends were inside in a nice warm place with food, wine, singing and dancing – he knew they'd be having a great time while he was stuck outside on sentry duty. And as the evening drew on he knew it would get cold. He could have kicked himself for getting landed with this job – all because the officer had found a tiny spot of rust on his sword during an inspection. 'You slovenly, scruffy, 'orrible little man!' he had roared. 'Guard duty every night for a week!'

So that was how Jake came to be outside while his comrades were whooping it up at the party. He was trying to think of some way he could have some fun and spoil the party for them when he noticed a tall shadowy figure approaching.

'Halt!' shouted Jake. 'Who goes there?'

'Samuel the prophet, with an urgent message for the commander of the guard,' came the reply.

'Have you any proof of identity?' asked the guard.

'Woof!' said Samuel's dog.

'That will do nicely, sir,' said Jake immediately. 'What is your message?'

'Foreign spies in the woods,' Samuel told him. 'They must be caught immediately.'

The guard was excited, but thought he'd better check.

'How d'you know they're spies?'

Samuel tried to sound impatient

'I heard them talking about it. Now do get a move on, before they escape.'

Jake thought this was wonderful! So his comrades thought they were going to have a good time while he was stuck outside did they? Not any more! He picked up the large bell in his sentry box and started to ring it as loudly as he could.

As the guard turned out, some of them still trying to swallow their food as they pulled on their helmets and buckled on their swords, Samuel explained to the guard commander where the 'spies' were. 'Well done, sir!' said the officer. 'You and your dog had better go ahead and lead us to them.'

As they set off, no one noticed a young, dark-eyed girl standing in the shadows near the barrack gate, and watching what was happening with intense interest.

Meanwhile, in the wood, Davey and Mr. fforbes were waiting anxiously.

'I just hope we are in time,' said the curator. 'It would be terrible if they were to do anything to that machine.'

Davey was more worried about being captured again. 'Can't we do something else?' he asked. 'Those soldiers looked very fierce to me.'

'It's the only way of getting to the time machine,' answered the curator. 'They are sure to be guarding it very closely.'

'Yes, but…'

'Trust me,' said Mr. fforbes, kindly. 'Have I let you down yet?'

That made Davey feel a little better, although not much. And he began to feel worse again when he saw flickering lights in the distance and heard the clamour of the approaching soldiers. As they drew nearer, the light of their flaming torches cast strange shadows and made them look even more fearsome than they were. Davey began to have even bigger doubts about Samuel's plan, but it was too late now – the guard had almost arrived. Samuel led the way with King, who was enjoying playing at being a tracker dog, and behind him came about twenty large, tough and extremely angry soldiers whose party had just been interrupted.

The curator pushed Davey down into the undergrowth and squatted beside him. 'Now stand up when I do,' he whispered, 'and pretend to be frightened.'

Pretend? This bit of acting would be easier than the school Nativity play – no pretending about it!

As Samuel and his dog got closer, Mr. fforbes stood up and Davey followed his example.

'Call off the dog! Call him off! It's a fair cop – we'll come quietly!' gibbered the curator.

'Don't ham it up,' Davey whispered. 'They only talk like that in old movies!'

'Don't be impertinent!' responded his companion, and then went back to pleading for mercy – not making a very convincing job of it in Davey's opinion. *He* would have done much better, he thought, because he wouldn't have been acting – except the bit about the dog.

Samuel pulled King back. The dog strained at the leash as he barked and howled, wanting to get to his new friends . To anyone not in the know, it was very convincing indeed! 'I'll hold the dog off,' Samuel called out, 'as long as you don't try to escape.'

'We won't, sir – honestly,' said Mr. fforbes, whose acting was definitely improving with practice.

'Right – get them!' rasped the guard commander, and the soldiers came forward, grabbed the two 'spies' and the whole company marched back toward the town.

When they got to the town it was in almost complete darkness which took Davey a little by surprise and made him realise just how much he took light for granted. Here there were no street lights, no well-lit shop fronts, no car headlamps or traffic lights. There was just the light from the soldiers' torches, and the occasional gleam of an oil lamp through a house window. The road they were walking along was really only a dirt track, hardened by the passing of thousands of pairs of feet over the years and baked hard by the sun. As they tramped along, stumbling in the occasional rut or pothole, the soldiers roughly pushed their captives from behind to keep them going.

Before long, they came to the barrack gate. The sentry on duty seemed a lot more cheerful than the soldiers who had arrested them. He seemed actually to be trying to suppress a grin, but Davey couldn't imagine why. As they walked past, the guard commander spoke sharply to him. 'Take that smirk off your face, soldier! If you're so happy I can always let you do some more sentry duty.'

The sentry's face immediately straightened, and the company of soldiers, with the two prisoners, the prophet and the dog, went through into the barracks courtyard. And still no one noticed the dark-eyed young girl standing in the shadows and watching intently.

'Thank you for your help, sir,' said the officer to Samuel.

'You're welcome,' Samuel replied, ' but before you…'

'That's all right, sir, leave them to us.'

Samuel tried again. 'I just think you ought to know…'

The officer knew his men would be keen to get back to what was left of their party, and didn't want to waste time gossiping.

'We'll take care of them, thank you sir,' he said. Then he chose two very large soldiers. 'Take them to the cage and tell those stupid guards to watch them carefully if they value their heads. The rest can fall out.'

The two guards pushed Davey and the curator across the courtyard and through a doorway into a large hall. Near the entrance was a rough wooden table where two guards were playing dice to pass the time. Down one side of the room were a row of cages made of stout iron bars with bolts and chains on the doors. Davey and the curator were led to an empty cage and pushed inside. The door slammed shut and was chained and bolted by the soldiers who told the guards what the officer had said.

'Yeah, yeah – anything else?' responded one of the guards wearily.

'Just don't say you weren't told, that's all.' And the soldiers left.

The other cages were occupied, and Davey recognised some of the Philistine captives he'd seen earlier. They were a sorry sight now, and simply looked on sullenly as the new prisoners were locked up, not even appearing to register the strange clothes they were wearing.

Davey and Mr. fforbes tried their best to make themselves comfortable on the hard, cold floor. They didn't expect to get much sleep here, and on top of that they were both very worried about what would happen tomorrow.

'Samuel didn't mention the machine,' Davey whispered to Mr. fforbes.

'Don't worry,' the curator assured him. 'I'm sure he'll see that they make the connection.'

Davey remembered what he had already witnessed the Israelites doing to their enemies. 'But what if they don't?' he insisted. 'What if they just decide to kill us straight away? You heard what happened – nobody listens to Samuel around here.'

Mr. fforbes couldn't convince Davey, who was very frightened and very angry,

'You and your clever ideas,' he said, 'Now *you've* got us into a Fine Mess!'

CHAPTER 12

The Dark-eyed Princess

The girl stood outside, watching through the window. There was a light near the prisoners, so that the guards could keep watch, and that meant that she could get a good look at these strange people. She studied the man's suit, his winged collar and bow tie, and then turned attention to the boy, who she thought must be three or four years younger than herself and was dressed differently from the older man, but equally oddly. It was obvious that they were from a place quite unlike anywhere she had been. Perhaps they came from a completely different world! The more she thought about it, the more convinced of that she became. Yes, of course, they had come here from somewhere very distant indeed, and they had used the strange chariot she had seen earlier to make the journey. What was it like, she wondered, this bizarre world? What did these truly amazing clothes mean? More to the point, what other wonders might there be in the world from which they had come?

The guards looked up from their game of dice as the girl entered the room. Davey and Mr. fforbes had noticed her as well, and watched to see what would happen.

'Good evening, Your Highness,' said one of the soldiers. 'I hope you'll forgive me for saying so, but I don't think the king would approve of your being here.'

The girl looked at the guard very calmly through her large, dark eyes. When she spoke, her voice was steady and the words flowed from her lips like music on the night air. 'I don't think he would approve of it if he knew you were asleep on duty last night, either – but who's going to tell him?'

The guard paled, and stammered. 'Oh-er-of-of-of course, Your-er-Your Highness, is there something I can do for you?

'I doubt it,' answered the girl, coolly. 'After all, you haven't seen me, have you?'

'No – certainly not, Your Highness,' replied the guard hastily.

'Excellent!' said the girl. 'And I didn't hear you snoring last night.'

The girl approached the cage where Davey and Mr. fforbes had listened with admiration to the whole exchange. As she got closer, Davey noticed what a very beautiful girl she was. She had golden skin, long dark hair and of course those eyes like two dark, mysterious pools. Her nose was straight, as though chiselled, above a pair of lips that turned upwards slightly at the corners, and seemed to give her a permanent hint of a smile, adding to her general air of mystery. The mouth opened.

'Hello,' she said. 'My name is Michal. Princess Michal.'

Davey was sure he had heard that name before somewhere else, but before he could think where, the curator spoke.

'Princess Michal? So you must be the daughter of…'

'King Saul. Precisely. And whom have I the pleasure of addressing?'

Davey thought Mr. fforbes was going to faint! Such elegant speech and bearing in one of her age! At last, the curator was thinking, in this dreadful barbaric place, here was someone who – even though so young – could hold a decent conversation!

Mr. fforbes couldn't be sure Samuel hadn't talked about them, so he replied carefully, 'My name is Mistaforbs, and this is my pupil, Davey.'

119

The girl's eyes opened wider for a moment, and she looked slightly alarmed. 'Davey? Davey? You aren't related to that dreadful little upstart everyone's been getting hysterical about, are you?'

Mr. fforbes nearly said, 'That dreadful little upstart is your future husband,' but stopped himself just in time.

'Oh, you mean David,' he said. 'No, they're not related. But what is so reprehensible about him?'

'Oh, he's quite tiresome,' answered the

Princess. 'When he arrived here he was full of how God had helped him kill Goliath – which of course is a matter of opinion; a lucky strike is how the experienced soldiers are describing it. Then tonight at the celebration, he insisted on singing some songs he's written and accompanying himself on a kind of home-made harp. I think he's going to be Very Difficult To Live With. But never mind that – I came here to find out about you.'

Mr. fforbes thought this might be their opportunity to make certain of things. So he whispered loudly to Davey, 'Whatever you do, don't tell her about the chariot.'

Davey played his part perfectly. 'You've been and gone and told her you old…'

'Don't be impertinent!' Mr. fforbes whispered, just as loudly. 'Anyway, she can't possibly have heard that.'

Of course, not only Princess Michal but the guards and possibly everybody else within a hundred metres *had* heard it. The princess looked as interested as Davey looked cross. 'Now what chariot would that be?' she asked, innocently.

'Oh, nothing,' replied the curator, looking just a little *too* innocent himself.

Princess Michal changed tack. 'Those are wonderful clothes you're wearing,' she commented. 'They don't look as though they were made here.'

Mr. fforbes blurted out. 'You are of course precisely correct; they were made in our own worl... oh dear!'

Turning to Davey, and looking very humble and apologetic, Mr. fforbes said, 'I'm sorry, Davey. I think we're going to have to tell her.'

'You may as well – you've blabbed just about everything already,' Davey replied.

The girls eyes had opened wider than ever and she said, 'What "world" would that be?'

Mr. fforbes spoke in a resigned sort of voice. 'Well, I suppose I'll have to tell you, but you must not tell anyone else, of course – especially your father.'

The girl crossed her fingers behind her back. 'Oh, of course not!' she said.

'Very well, then,' said Mr. fforbes. 'We have come from another world; a world completely unknown here, and many years' journey away.'

The large, dark eyes opened wider still.

'In this world,' the curator went on, 'We have many wonderful things. We can travel across several countries in one day and not even feel tired.'

'Huh, that's what you think!' thought Davey, whose parents had recently taken him to Spain on holiday. 'Six hours' delay in an airport departure lounge and you'd be tired all right!'

Mr. fforbes went on. 'We have buildings large enough to contain your entire town! We have power that can light a dark room or warm a cold one, just like that!' He snapped his fingers dramatically.

The girl was looking more and more amazed, and Davey joined in.

'Yes, and we've learned how to fly through the air,' he said, '*and* live under water.'

Davey had gone too far. 'I don't believe you,' the girl said. 'You must think I'm stupid.'

'But it's true,' Davey said. 'And we have moving pictures, too, that we can send through the air to places on the other side of the world.'

The girl's earlier look of wide-eyed wonder had changed to anger. 'I will teach you not to mock an Israelite princess!' she said, and turned to go.

'Of course, we can prove this to you,' Mr. fforbes called out.

The girl stopped, slowly turned round and walked back to them.

'All our secrets are in the chariot,' said the curator. 'But only we know how to release them.'

This made the princess think again. Her father would be very interested in the secrets of the chariot. If what these people said was true, their knowledge could make King Saul the most powerful ruler in the world, and that might stop the upstart David from getting big ideas. She might get into a little trouble by admitting she'd been talking to the prisoners, but it would be worth it for the reward she would get for the information.

She turned to leave, stopping on the way to pull the desk from under the now dozing guards who fell in a heap on the floor and got up looking very embarrassed.

'I'd stay awake if I were you,' she said. 'If those two got away you might not live to regret it.'

CHAPTER 13

The Escape

The night seemed to go on for ever, but eventually daylight came and they heard the marching feet of a squad of soldiers who stopped outside the outer door. The officer came in and said, 'Release those two – I'm to take them to the king.'

Davey and Mr. fforbes were then led outside, placed between the ranks of soldiers and marched off across the square and into a building on the other side. All the time, Mr. fforbes was looking around trying to get a glimpse of the time machine, but it was nowhere in sight.

King Saul was a most impressive figure. He was tall, handsome and sported the same kind of bushy beard that so many of his men seemed to have. No longer in battledress, he wore a long purple robe which came down almost to the floor and had golden fringes around the cuffs and ankles. From a gold chain round his neck hung his seal of office, and his fingers were heavy with jewelled rings.

'All right, you can go,' he said to the guards. 'I don't think these two are any threat to me.'

The guards looked doubtful, but the king glowered at them and they scuttled away very quickly.

That's better!' said the king. 'When you're in my position you learn not to trust anybody – don't want them hearing what you're going to tell me.'

'And just what are we going to tell you?' asked the curator.

'Now don't play games with me, Mistaforbs!' said the king. 'Yes, you see, I already know all about you, so let's get to the point. I want the secret of your special chariot.'

'What if we don't want to tell?' asked Davey, impetuously.

'Why, then,' answered the king, 'we do with you what we do with all spies.' He smiled, ominously. 'It's very amusing – but unfortunately not so funny when you're on the receiving end.'

'We're not spies, Your Majesty,' answered the curator. 'We are philosophers.'

That was the first time anyone had called Davey a name like that, but he let it pass.

Mr. fforbes continued, 'My pupil and I wish only to learn from great civilisations such as yours, so that our world may benefit from your example.'

The king's eyes twinkled. 'So you have come to share knowledge?' he asked.

'Precisely, Your Majesty, replied the curator, 'for the mutual enhancement of our great civilisations.'

The king looked at Davey.

'I think he means we'll all do well out of it,' Davey translated.

'That being so, said the king triumphantly, 'you have already done much better than we have. You have seen our civilisation. Now you must do your part. You will please give me the secret of the chariot. If you do not, I shall have you killed – and it will be a particularly horrible and entertaining death. But of course, it is entirely up to you. Do not allow me to put any pressure upon you.'

King Saul turned away and began peeling an orange while humming tunelessly to himself.

Davey had suspected all along that this had not been one of Mr. fforbes's better ideas, and now he was quite sure of it.

'With respect, Your Majesty,' the curator began. Davey had heard television interviewers say that, and he knew it meant the exact opposite. Saul seemed to have guessed that too, for he frowned very severely.

'If you kill us,' Mr. fforbes went on, 'you will never learn the secret of the chariot. But we are quite willing to share it with you. The only problem is that it cannot be described except to someone who already understands it – that is the difficulty with any scientific discussion. It must be demonstrated.'

The king was not happy about this; it seemed rather risky. Then he had an idea.

Does the boy understand the chariot?' he

asked. 'Would he be able to demonstrate it?'

Mr. fforbes understood the question.

'Certainly, Your Majesty,' he answered. 'My pupil is well able to reveal the mysteries of our non-equestrian conveyance.'

King Saul looked at Davey.

Davey shrugged.

'Horseless chariot,' explained Mr. fforbes impatiently

'Very well, then,' replied the king. 'He will show us the secrets of the chariot, and you will remain my hostage. At least I can understand what he says!'

Davey didn't like the way the wind was blowing at all. 'I-I-I can't!' he stammered. And Saul looked positively ferocious.

'My pupil is a little inexperienced,' put in Mr. fforbes hastily. 'He will only be able to operate it if I am there to supervise him.

Seeing the king's suspicious look, Mr. fforbes added, 'In inexperienced hands the magical power unleashed could be very dangerous. I'm afraid I really must be there.'

Now Saul of course should not have been interested in playing around with magic since it was strictly against his religion, but the curator knew that a little thing like that wouldn't stop him – he would always go against his religion if he thought it would increase his power. Saul was more concerned about the danger that these two strange characters might try to escape, but he couldn't see any other way so he eventually agreed. Just in case, though, he took two large soldiers to guard Mr. fforbes as he led them out of the room and through the barracks to a high wall in which was a small door. Passing through, they found themselves in a courtyard surrounded by high walls. And there, shining in the morning sun, and to Mr. fforbes's relief apparently in one piece, was the time machine. The heavy gates at one end were left securely closed, and the two guards held on very firmly to Mr. fforbes's arms as Davey climbed into the machine.

'My pupil will now prepare the chariot to release its secrets,' said the curator. Davey turned the key while the king held his breath, not knowing what to expect. As before, nothing happened for a few seconds, and King Saul was beginning to get impatient.

'If you are trying to deceive me...'

His voice tailed off as the computer screen started to glow. As the shapes and shadows began to appear, the king stepped forward excitedly.

'I urge Your Majesty not to touch the chariot,' said Mr. fforbes quickly. 'Its power is truly awesome, and only those who know its secret may safely approach.'

By now the programme had loaded and the on-screen message appeared.

Time/space co-ordinate software,
copyright © Prof. H. I. Hipperwattle
Last co-ordinates
AD1995/1506/1352/5343N/0151W/+0143
F4 for list of last six co-ordinates
F5 to set new co-ordinates
RETURN to return

Davey's heart was pounding very fast; he knew that this was the crucial moment, but the curator was firmly held by the two large soldiers. He must have plan for getting into the time machine, but what was it? Davey dared not press RETURN until Mr. fforbes was safely inside.

King Saul was peering at the screen in amazement. What was this device, and from where had this writing appeared? More to the point what on earth could it all mean? Mr. fforbes was pretty confident that he could never even guess at the answer, but thought it best not to take any chances. Although still in the grip of the two guards, he knew that the time had come for a massive gamble. He cleared his throat to attract the king's attention.

'I shall now ask my pupil to perform the final ritual, and then the chariot will reveal the secrets of its power,' he said very gravely. 'Now, Davey, you remember what you did last time, don't you?'

Davey thought that was a clear signal to go

ahead, so he looked at Mr. fforbes who nodded vigorously, and then at the king and the two soldiers who were looking very anxious indeed, and reached out his hand to press RETURN.

The same noises began again that he had heard in the museum cellar. First the whirring sound which made the Israelites look distinctly worried, and then the pop-pop-popping which made their eyebrows disappear into their headbands. When the 'thumpety thump' started, they began to edge away from the machine and no sooner had the siren begun to wail than the three of them turned tail and fled, dragging Mr. fforbes with them. Davey thought it was all going wrong again, but he need not have worried. As soon as the curator began to struggle the guards got their priorities sorted out and let him go so that they could escape quickly.

By now, Davey was getting alarmed. The courtyard had begun to spin around them and he was sure Mr. fforbes had left it too late. He had underestimated him yet again! The curator turned and ran at great speed toward the machine. With a thud, he landed breathlessly in the passenger seat, and said, 'Thank goodness I shall never have to do that again!'

But he was wrong.

CHAPTER 14

Stowaway

As the courtyard spun faster around them, Davey and the curator breathed a sigh of relief. It had not been easy, but they had managed to get the time machine back and escape and – as far as they could tell – no damage had been done to history. Soon, the noise had stopped and the spinning landscape had become a blur. Mr. fforbes took the opportunity to impress upon Davey once more the vital importance of keeping the machine secret.

The blur was slowing down. Out of curiosity, the two time travellers looked out for glimpses of familiar scenes, but with no success. After all, things were still going past at a great speed. Then the spinning slowed down even more and they got ready to leave the machine. The museum cellar would be a very welcome sight. But what was happening? The cellar looked different. It was bigger, brighter and full of people whom they didn't know at all. As the machine came to rest they heard a voice cry out, 'Cut! Cut! Cut! What the blue blazes is going on here? Why can't Special Effects *ever* get *anything* right!'

Davey and the curator looked around them and found that they appeared to be on a film set. A hysterical little man in his shirt sleeves was shouting at everybody and demanding to know what was going on, and a bemused cameraman was scratching his head and saying, 'There's nothing in the script about this.'

A group of people in costume (probably actors and actresses) suddenly burst into a round of applause. 'Quite the best stunt that I've ever seen!' someone said.

The director wasn't so impressed. 'Clear the stage!' he yelled. 'Everybody out! Somebody call Security.'

'Where are we?' asked Davey?

'What's happened to the museum?' gasped the curator.

Davey was about to say that the time

machine must have gone wrong when they heard a familiar feminine voice say, 'So this is your world! It's certainly different!'

Davey and Mr. fforbes turned to look behind them and there, gradually emerging from behind the seats was the beautiful but unwelcome face of Princess Michal.

'What on earth!' exclaimed the curator. 'How did you get here?'

'Oh, it was no trouble,' said the princess airily. 'I can go anywhere I like – I can always get round sentries – so I just hid in the chariot early this morning.'

'You Ridiculous Child!' fumed Mr. fforbes. 'So this Fine Mess is all your fault!'

Davey was amazed. 'You mean that, because she didn't stay behind, that's why the museum's gone?'

'Not gone,' his companion corrected him. 'It's never been built. The whole of history is different because she didn't marry David. People who would have been born haven't been, and events that would have happened haven't happened – and the long-term effect of all that is that the whole of history has changed. It's only by sheer luck that you and I still exist.'

Princess Michal was looking around, quite unaware of the effect she had had. Her beautiful dark eyes became bigger and darker with every new thing she saw. 'It's wonderful!' she breathed. 'What are all these strange sculptures – are they your gods?'

'No, they're cameras.' said Davey. 'They make the moving pictures I told you about.'

'Never mind all that,' hissed the curator. 'We've got to get out of here before we get into more trouble.'

Too late! Trouble was already approaching in the form of the film director and some very heavy looking security guards.

Quickly, Davey turned the key and the computer screen glowed.

'Where are we going now?' asked the princess.

'Somewhere even more exciting than this,' lied the curator. 'Now stay still, because this is very dangerous.'

When Davey was about to press RETURN, Mr. fforbes stopped him and pressed 'F5'. Immediately a flashing cursor appeared in the line of co-ordinates. The curator moved it along the line and changed two of the figures before pressing RETURN. As the machine started up, the security guards stopped and stared in confusion. Then they began to walk backwards at increasing speed. Soon, everything was a blur again and the three occupants of the time machine relaxed.

'What have you done?' Davey asked the curator.

'I'm taking us back to precisely one day before we first arrived in the past,' explained the curator. 'Then we can get this Silly Girl back to her home and hopefully things will go on correctly from there.'

Princess Michal didn't really know what was going on, but she wasn't very happy about it. 'Get me back?' she said. 'You said we were going somewhere better.'

'Precisely,' agreed Mr. fforbes. 'And for an awful

lot of people this will be a great deal better!'

When the machine stopped again, they were back where they had first landed. The curator turned to Davey. 'I'm going to get this Ridiculous Child back to the town,' he said. 'It is imperative that she arrives safely. As soon as I get back here, we must go, so leave the computer running. And whatever you do, *do not wander off.*'

Princess Michal was furious. 'You're not taking me back there,' she said. 'I shall refuse to go.'

She had reckoned without Mr. fforbes's extraordinary fitness and skill. Rather than stop to argue, he simply grasped the girl's arm and set off again on the rocky climb. Davey watched in wonder as he scrambled from rock to rock, as he had done earlier, but this time dragging a very unwilling and angry Princess Michal behind him.

'If I were you, you Silly Girl,' the curator gasped, 'I'd stop struggling because if I am compelled to let you go you will certainly be injured in the fall.' Although she was furious with him, Princess Michal had to admit to herself that he was right. So she agreed a temporary truce while they climbed the steep rocks. When they were safely at the top, however, she started again, but Mr. fforbes was ready for her. He took a firmer grip upon her arm and continued along the track where he and Davey had watched the victory procession. When they were as close to the town as he dared go he turned to the princess.

'I am most truly sorry, Your Highness,' he

said, 'but it was necessary. There is your home, and I suggest you go to it without delay.'

Princess Michal was furious! 'Right! she said vindictively. 'If you won't take me to your world, you will have to stay in mine.'

Then she ran up the road toward the town as fast as her legs would carry her, shouting at the top of her voice and waving her arms about. The sentry on the gate recognised her and called out the guard, and before he knew what had happened Mr. fforbes found himself being pursued by a gang of heavily armed and very angry soldiers.

Back at the machine, Davey was getting anxious. There had been quite enough adventure in this escapade to last him for a lifetime, and he would be very much happier when Mr. fforbes got back and they could take off. Then he pricked up his ears: it sounded as though a large number of people were on the way, and judging by their shouts they were not delivering invitations to a tea party. Davey strained his eyes upwards and eventually saw the curator half scrambling, half falling down the rock face with a look of absolute terror on his face. Every so often, he would slip, jarring himself painfully and sending a shower of stones to land around the time machine. And not far behind him, the soldiers were doing the same. This time, Mr. fforbes' unusual agility did not seem to be helping him quite so much. He, of course, had already done a strenuous climb, and the soldiers were younger than he was and more used to the terrain. Every moment they were getting closer, and Davey thought they were bound to catch him. What would happen then? But what was going on? The soldiers had stopped chasing Mr. fforbes and were scrambling back up the steep hill as fast as they possibly could. Mr. fforbes, of course, did not know that, and was continuing his painful and undignified descent. Davey looked around to see what had frightened the soldiers, and when he saw it his blood ran cold.

There, swaggering into view round the bend in the track, was the unmistakable figure of the man-mountain, Goliath. At first, Davey was confused until he realised that they had gone back to the day *before* the battle. Goliath of course would not recognise Davey, but attacking anything that wasn't a Philistine was second nature to him. So he stopped only for a moment to get over the shock before he let out a bellow and started to run toward the machine.

Davey knew it would be touch and go. His first thought was to press RETURN and get away, but he knew he could not leave Mr. fforbes in that predicament. He waited until he thought Mr. fforbes was close enough, and struck the key. The noise which the time machine made sounded to Davey like the sweetest music he had ever heard! Even as it increased, though it could not drown the shouts of rage coming from Goliath who was now running very fast indeed and looking extremely dangerous.

Just as the scenery began to spin, the curator fell the last few feet, staggered up to the time machine and threw himself into the seat beside

Davey. By then, Goliath was also only a few paces away and grasped hold of the time machine in an attempt to stop it. However, he succeeded only in tearing the bonnet off the front of the machine before it disappeared into the mists of the ages. As the giant fell away, still safely in his own time, the curator sank down exhausted in his seat.

'Three times!' he gasped. 'Three times you have caused me to exert myself in that fashion. I sincerely hope there will not be a fourth!'

CHAPTER 15

Back to the Present

The final journey was reassuring. Before the fast-forward became a blur, Davey caught a glimpse of a wedding and recognised the happy couple as David and Princess Michal. That should mean that things were back to what he regarded as 'normal'.

During the blur phase, Davey found himself looking in admiration at the curator. When they first met, he would never have believed that this man was so resourceful. Mr. fforbes, for his part, despite the grazes and bruises he was nursing, found himself almost regretting that they were going back. For all the problems he had caused, the boy was really quite a Good Lad At Heart, and life was certainly going to be duller without him around. Mr. fforbes secretly hoped Davey would come to the museum again, but vowed to make doubly sure that the cellar was kept locked.

When the scenery began to slow down, they saw familiar scenes again, but this time going forwards. They saw a large ship strike an iceberg and go down beneath the waves; they saw aircraft taking off, rain falling from clouds. It looked as though this time they had got it right.

Sure enough, as the scene slowed and stopped, they recognised the walls of the museum cellar with the dim light coming from the high window and showing up the shelves of broken pottery. The curator reached across in front of Davey and removed the key from the machine. 'I think that will be safer with me from now on,' he said, 'and I'll take your STUART bracelet back as well. Thank you. Now you go upstairs first. I will follow and see that the door is locked.'

When Davey emerged into the main part of the museum it was as though he had never been away. Miss Wilkins was explaining the contents of the first room; Pompous was staring blissfully at her, and Miss Thompson was glaring balefully at Pompous. Everything was back to normal. Davey heard a voice in his ear. 'Just thank your lucky stars we have not changed history after all. That would have been a Fine Mess.' And Mr. fforbes disappeared into his office, picking up sweet papers as he went and fussing under his breath. Davey pretended to be rejoining the group, but sneaked back toward the curator's office. He wanted to see where those keys were put.

By the time Davey finally got back to the party of children, they had moved on to the next room and Miss Wilkins was explaining what was in a display case. Davey could not see the display from where he was, but he could clearly hear Miss Wilkins's voice. 'This is a Very Interesting Item,' she said. 'It was excavated in the Holy Land in the nineteenth century. No one knows exactly what it is, but it is thought to be some sort of primitive shield used in battle.'

Edwin Harrington's voice piped up. 'That ain't nothin' of the sort, Miss. You're 'avin' us on!'

Pompous nearly had a fit, and Miss Wilkins went a little pink as she said, 'I assure you I am not "having you on". That is what we believe it to be.'

'Oh, go on, Miss – pull the other one,' the

shrill voice rejoined. 'That's the bonnet off of a nineteen seventy MG Midget, that is. I know 'cos my mum used to 'ave one – she's mad about old cars, she is – only me Dad made 'er change it for a Cortina.'

By now, all the children were laughing, and Miss Wilkins looked very embarrassed. 'I know it looks remarkably similar,' she said. 'All the same, it has been examined by the world's best experts and they really should know.'

'He's right, Miss,' came another embarrassing voice. 'Look, you can see the catch to hold it closed.'

Pompous decided at that point that it would probably be best to put off any further tour of the museum until another time – perhaps after the children moved up to their next school.

'Come along, children,' he said. 'I think we'll go back now.'

When Davey got home, Mum was waiting, and she wasn't pleased. 'What *have* you done to your clothes?' she asked. 'You look as though you've been mountaineering or something. If this is what happens on school outings you'd better not go no any more.'

'Oh, no!' said Davey. 'Please let me go again, History's really ace!' For some reason, his mother had a sudden urge to sit down on the nearest chair.

'We'll talk about it later,' said Mum, struggling to her feet. 'Go and watch telly while I get us all a meal.'

'Do I have to?' asked Davey. 'I'd rather go and read if that's all right. Can I borrow the encyclopaedia?'

It was really rather a waste: Mum had only just stood up, and now she had to sit down again. Suddenly, she felt much too tired and stressed to cook, and she picked up the telephone to order some pizzas to be delivered.

Jenny soon came in from school and a little later Dad got home from work, and they all sat down together to eat.

'Davey enjoyed his museum visit today, didn't you darling?' said Mum (who was still getting over the shocks she had had). 'Would you like to tell us all about it?'

There was nothing Davey would like more, but he knew he couldn't – and anyway they wouldn't believe him. He'd just get into trouble for making up stories. So he simply said, 'Well, it was very exciting, and I want to study history and science when I'm older.'

'You? Study?' scoffed Jenny through a mouthful of pizza. 'You don't know the meaning of the word. I bet you haven't learnt a thing all day.'

'I've learnt one thing,' retorted Davey. 'I've learnt that just because you're bigger it doesn't make you better – so next time there's some washing up to be done, *you* can do it. And don't talk with your mouth full.'

Jenny was so shocked that she didn't know what to say at first. By the time she'd thought of an answer, Davey was talking again.

'Mum, what was that protest rally about today?'

'Eat your pizza,' said Dad, quickly.

'Oh, it was about the plans to close our local hospital,' said Mum.

'Don't go filling the boy's head with all your loonie left nonsense,' said Dad. 'The council must know what they're doing.'

'Rubbish!' retorted Mum. 'The nearest accident and emergency department will be ten miles away – a fat lot of good if you're bleeding to death.'

Dad smiled in a fatherly kind of way at his wife and said, 'I know you mean well, dear, but you see it's all about Power. The council have the Power and they can do Whatever They Like.'

Davey interrupted. 'I think you should go on fighting it, Mum. After all, the little people can win sometimes. You know – like David and Goliath.'

'Hmph!' snorted Dad. 'That's the trouble with Young People Today: they've got no Experience Of Life, and they think they know it all. Shut up and eat your pizza.'